KU-264-379

PUFFIN BOOKS

Published by the Penguin Group
Penguin Books Ltd, 27 Wrights Lane, London W8 5TZ, England
Penguin Putnam Inc., 375 Hudson Street, New York, New York 10014, USA
Penguin Books Australia Ltd, Ringwood, Victoria, Australia
Penguin Books Canada Ltd, 10 Alcorn Avenue, Toronto, Ontario, Canada M4V 3B2
Penguin Books (NZ) Ltd, Private Bag 102902, NSMC, Auckland, New Zealand

Penguin Books Ltd, Registered Offices: Harmondsworth, Middlesex, England

On the World Wide Web at: www.penguin.com

First published by Hamish Hamilton 1999
Published in Puffin Books 2000
1 3 5 7 9 10 8 6 4 2

Text copyright © John Yeoman, 1999
Illustrations copyright © Quentin Blake, 1999
All rights reserved

The moral right of the author and illustrator has been asserted

Made and printed in Italy by Printer Trento Srl

Except in the United States of America, this book is sold subject to the condition that
it shall not, by way of trade or otherwise, be lent, re-sold, hired out, or otherwise circulated
without the publisher's prior consent in any form of binding or cover other than
that in which it is published and without a similar condition including
this condition being imposed on the subsequent purchaser

British Library Cataloguing in Publication Data
A CIP catalogue record for this book is available from the British Library

ISBN 0–140–56512–4

John Yeoman

The Heron and the Crane

Illustrated by Quentin Blake

PUFFIN BOOKS

Coventry City Libraries
Schools' Library Service

PET

Once upon a time, in a swamp, there lived a heron and a crane.

They didn't live together: the heron had built her scrappy nest on a dry mound at one end of the swamp, and the crane had built his, which looked very much the same, at the other end.

One day, as the crane was standing gazing at himself in the shallow muddy water, it occurred to him that he was rather lonely.

He scratched the back of his right leg with his left foot for a while, and then said to himself, "It's high time that I got married." But who could be his wife?

It didn't take him long to decide on the heron, because she was the only unmarried bird who was roughly the same shape and size as he was. There were some elderly lady ducks, but they were out of the question.

And so, after grooming himself very carefully, the crane stepped gracefully through the still water until he came to the other end of the swamp, where the heron lived.

"Good morning, Heron," said the crane, feeling a little embarrassed because, although he had been thinking hard on his walk, he still hadn't quite decided how to put his suggestion.

"Good morning, Crane," replied the heron, who had no idea why he was visiting her. "Won't you come in?" She took a step backwards to make room for him to stand on the edge of her nest. She would have invited him to sit down but there wouldn't have been room for all the legs.

"Will you marry me?" asked the crane suddenly.

He had meant to lead up to this subject rather gradually, but in his excitement he couldn't think of anything else to say.

The heron was very taken aback: she just wasn't prepared for such a question. She lost her head and cried, "Marry you! Goodness gracious, what a ridiculous idea! Just look at you: you're all legs and neck! And those awful knobbly knees!"

The crane was very hurt by this outburst. He cast a sad look over his shoulder at his knees. They *were* rather bony.

"And what's more, you just couldn't keep me in fish!"

She shouted this so loudly that he knew it was time to go.
Without a backward glance he turned and made his way
slowly through the swamp to his own nest at the other end.

When he had disappeared from view the heron thought it over. She was very unhappy about the way she'd behaved.

"I've been very unkind to insult him like that," she thought. "And as for the fish, well, I'm perfectly capable of catching my own."

So she decided to go and apologize to the crane and offer to marry him after all.

She left her nest and picked her way gracefully through the swamp water, hanging down her head very coyly as she approached the crane. He was standing rather sulkily with his back to her, but it was obvious that he had heard her coming.

"Crane!" she called softly.

He didn't answer.

"Crane!" she called. "I've come to apologize. I didn't really mean all those nasty things I said, and I take them all back."

He didn't move.

"Crane, it would make me very happy to become your wife."

On hearing this the crane turned round and gave her a
stony stare. "Thank you very much for your kind offer," he said,
"but, as you previously remarked, I don't want an extra beak to
feed. I'm sorry, but marriage between us is out of the question."

There was a moment of complete silence over the swamp before the heron burst into floods of tears and hurried off back to her own nest.

When she was out of sight the crane thought it over to himself, and suddenly felt very miserable.

"Why was I so cruel?" he said. "I want to marry her and now I've hurt her feelings. There's nothing for it; I shall just have to go and apologize for my behaviour."

He really did feel very ashamed of himself and, to make up for it, he caught a juicy frog which he carried dangling by one leg from his beak.

He stepped hastily through the swamp and stopped a little way from the heron's nest. He was so agitated that the frog was quivering.

"Heron," he mumbled nervously, "I'm sorry for what I said a little while ago, and I have brought you …"

The heron didn't give him time to finish. Her pride had been wounded and now she was in quite a temper. "I don't want your pity, you brute!" she screeched. "I know your sort. I would rather remain alone until the end of my days than marry someone as hard-hearted as you!"

This wasn't the welcome the crane had hoped for. His beak half opened in dismay and the frog fell with a plop into the wet mud.

"This is the end then," he thought to himself, and turned to make his way back to the other end of the swamp.

When he had gone the heron said to herself, "How sad he looked. I'm afraid I punished him too severely. I do so want to marry him. And what if he should do something terrible! Why, he may even throw himself into the swamp and drown!"

This was not really likely as the swamp water was nowhere more than ankle deep and the crane was a rather large bird. But the idea was enough to terrify the heron.

She almost ran to the other end of the swamp to reassure herself that the crane was still alive.

When she arrived she gasped breathlessly, "Oh, Crane, thank goodness you're safe. Please say you forgive me for my ..."

The crane interrupted her. "Oh, I've seen these moods of yours before. One minute you're as meek as a water vole and the next you're screeching your head off at me. No thank you, I'm ..."

And before he could finish she had turned and walked away, back to her own nest at the other end of the swamp.

And if you happen to go there, you'll probably find them still at it. Do you think they'll ever make up their minds?

3 8002 00865 7084

Significant Author